Picture the
World

Children's Art around the Globe

Tracy V Spates

MILET

Winter Beauty

Shmelev Nickolai (age 14)

Acknowledgements

My heartfelt thanks go out to the many people who have given so generously of their time and knowledge, to those who have offered their loving support and ideas, and to those who have contributed their creative talents to the making of this book.

Thank you, first, to the Semester-at-Sea Program of the University of Pittsburgh, for facilitating one of the most profound experiences of my life – truly a voyage of discovery – that has taught me a deep respect and appreciation for other cultures in our world. In particular I am grateful to Jill Wright, who believed in and supported my Children's Art Project from the start.

Thank you, next, to the children's organisations around the world and all the people who facilitated the wonderful art in this book: Joyce M Lane and Amanda Murray, and their students in Kyoto, Japan; Scott McKinney and his students (in particular Lesley Mattson and Lindsay Vaughn), who met with children in Quito, Ecuador; Henry Thiagaraj and the children of the Dalit Liberation Education Trust in Chennai, India; the Desai family in Gujurat, India; the Gupta family in Mumbai, India; Karen Mount and Kathy Meyer for sharing their art from Russia; Ayfer Goksen and the children of the Co Cuk Esirgeme Kurumu Orphanage in Istanbul, Turkey; Sister Didi

A Giitika and the children of the Ananda Marga Mission Academy in Mombasa, Kenya; Patrick Mabonga and the children of the SOS Children's Village in Mombasa, Kenya; Children's Hours School in Geneva, New York; and the Hy Vong 8 School for the Deaf in Ho Chi Minh City, Vietnam.

Thank you, also, to those who shared their knowledge of other cultures with me, helping to enrich and enliven the information for each country: James Henry Holland; Jack and Deb Harris; Manisha Desai; Lidia Pacira; Raymond Steifel; Kathleen Meyer; Judith and Angela McKinney; Heather Conners; Peace 4 Turtle Island (www.peace4turtleisland.org); and Sedat Turhan.

My heartfelt appreciation goes to Patricia Billings of Milet for her positive encouragement and continuous support.

To Virginia Tilley, who first put me in touch with Milet Publishing, goes special thanks. Also, to Toby Beckman for her exquisite quilt creations on pages 56 and 57, many thanks.

To Catherine Tidnam and Mariette Jackson goes my deep gratitude for their kindness, wisdom and patience in teaching me about the world of design and editing.

Thank you, finally, to my dear family and friends, who have believed in and supported this project from the very beginning, and with whose encouragement, love, patience and humour this book has become a reality: Mark and Maria VanTilburg; Kate Bullen; Claudette Columbus; Betsy Sterling Benjamin; my terrific children, Jamie and Lauren Spates; and my greatest and most adored fan, my husband, Jim, whose lovely photographs grace so many pages of this book.

30

Russia

36

Turkey

44

Kenya

50

USA

58

Vietnam

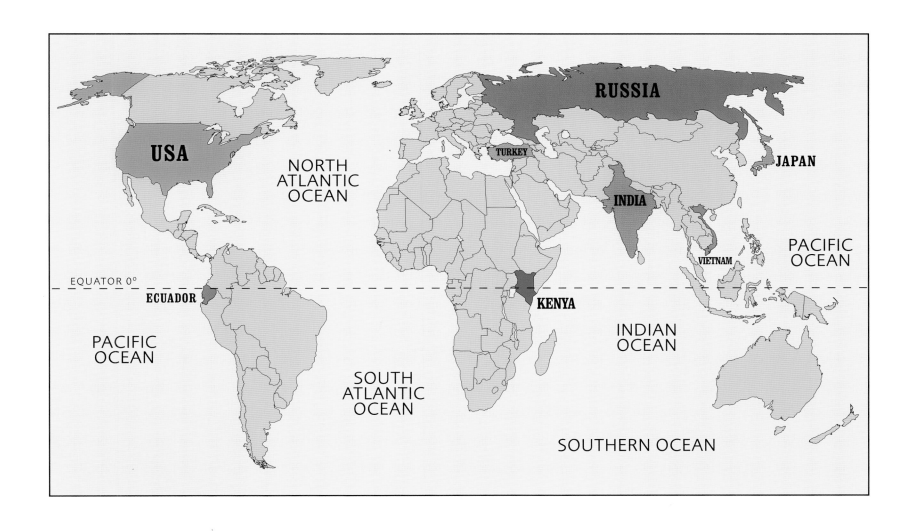

Introduction

Everywhere these days, people are seeing the world as a 'global community'. This view becomes especially important when we think of our children, for it is vital that we find ways to help them become aware of that larger community as they make their way towards their place in its future. Fortunately, young people are naturally eager and interested in understanding what it would be like to live in other countries. They want to learn about how others – particularly other young people – act, think, dress, and express themselves creatively.

This book aims to provide a bridge for this kind of learning. I have written it so that the children reading and looking at its pages will be able to readily identify with their peers around the world. The most important element in this process – the focus of the book – is the children's art from the eight countries we visit. As children turn the pages, they will see in the artistic expressions of other young people things that are familiar and shared and things that are unique and different.

In these pages, I have been able to combine my life-long passion for teaching art to children with my excitement for sharing what I have learned while visiting other countries. On three separate occasions, I have had the good fortune to travel around the world with the Semester-at-Sea Program, sponsored by the University of Pittsburgh in Pennsylvania. Returning to my classroom after each voyage, I was delighted to find that my students responded with great interest and enthusiasm to the activities and artefacts I brought back with me.

During my most recent voyage around the world, I was able to meet children in the ports we visited, and share art activities with them. Thus it was that, in schools, hospitals and orphanages, art became our international language of communication. In the pictures they so enthusiastically created, the children shared stories of their lives and cultures. Everywhere, I was moved and inspired by their hopeful and optimistic vision, even when it was clear that many of them were living extremely hard lives – often in poverty, sometimes in sickness.

After my return to the USA, I exhibited the artwork as part of a larger exhibition of children's art from around the world. I included photographs and examples of folk art from each country. I also gave workshops, where children created art reflecting a unique and characteristic technique from one of the countries. The exhibition and workshop were called 'Children and Art: The Global Connection', and the response from the public was overwhelmingly positive. To reach a larger audience and to share the treasures of the exhibition, I began to think about the possibility of a book.

It is my sincere hope that this book will be a springboard for further exploration, that it will inspire children and adults alike to learn about and appreciate the diversity of nations and peoples. I hope that together we can attempt to bring our 'global community' into full being – a world in which a deeper understanding of, and respect for, our similarities and differences will lead to a better world for everyone – especially for our children!

Tracy V. Spates

How to use this book

A note to parents and teachers

This book has been created for children of all ages everywhere. With art as its main focus, it is my hope that teachers and parents will discover in it a wonderful way to learn and teach about other places in our world.

Eight countries are visited on this world tour. In each case, children's art is showcased. The children's work presents an opportunity for storytelling and for discussing the similarities and differences between cultures. Also, the variety of art techniques used in the children's pictures offers a focus on both familiar and new ways of being creative.

Alongside the art, there are photographs of people and places to illustrate each country. These photos of homes, nature, families and friends, of people at work and at play, present further possibilities for connecting, and for sharing what life is like in other countries. Examples of local folk art are included to highlight some of the creative traditions in these countries. In some cases, there will be a noticeable connection between the folk art and the children's art.

At the beginning of each section, you will notice that the country's name is given both in English and in the main language of the country*. I have also included a phonetic spelling of the word (with capital letters indicating the stressed syllable/s), so you can try to pronounce it together.

The brief text descriptions, sometimes linking the photographs and the art, offer further insights into that country.

Finally, at the end of each section you will find a 'hands-on' step-by-step art activity. Each lesson is designed as a creative art activity for any age (younger children may require some supervision and help getting set up). For each lesson I have included information on the method and spirit of the folk art technique. Playing music during the art activity greatly enhances the experience. Some specific selections have been suggested for each country though there are many other global music recordings to chose from. It is important to mention that lessons are designed to encourage a maximum of freedom, fun and creativity!

*The USA section is an exception to this. As the main language here is English, the Native American Mohawk translation has been given instead.

*Prince and Princess Dolls
at Peach Blossom Festival*
Masae Asada (age 5)

Japan

日本

You pronounce this:
NEE Hohn

Mount Fuji is Japan's most sacred volcano.

Japan, sometimes called the Land of the Rising Sun, consists of over 6,500 volcanic islands off the far-eastern coast of Asia. A number of the volcanoes, like Mount Aso, are still active, and the country sometimes experiences earthquakes. Bridges and tunnels link the four main islands – Hokkaido, Honshu, Shikoku and Kyushu. If you took the train from Kobe to Tokyo – two cities on Honshu, the largest island – you would pass through forests of pine, cedar and bamboo, and paddy fields of rice. You might also get a glimpse of Japan's highest peak, snow-topped Mount Fuji, which is an inactive volcano.

The children who made these works of art come from Kyoto.

Living in harmony and with gentleness is an important part of Japanese life because there are so many people living in a small land area. Politeness is expected in all your encounters. You might greet someone on the street by bowing, bending slowly with your hands in front and dropping your head. One practice that emphasises these themes of harmony and politeness is the tea ceremony, or Chanoyu. This ancient ritual, a formal celebration of courtesy, order and beauty, is still widely practiced in Japan.

The kimono, belted with an obi, is still worn by both men and women on special occasions.

Season Clock
Yasushi Miyazaki (age 10)

Zen monks spend their time in prayer and meditation. People come to Buddhist temples and Shinto shrines to pray and meditate, and to attach paper wishes to trees, or perform ancient ceremonies and rituals. The beauty of the arching roofs, the stillness on the ground and the sweet smell of incense make these buildings very peaceful places to visit.

All Japanese people belong to the indigenous Shinto religion and 75% of the population are also Buddhist. Folk religion, with its gods, guardians and demons, is also an important part of Japanese life. Buddha is revered as a god-like teacher. He and many of the Shinto and folk gods teach wisdom and respect for all living things.

Japanese children go to school from April to March. However, they do have many holidays throughout the year. Hin-Matsuri, the Peach Blossom Festival, or Girl's Day, is in March and is a day when girls bring special dolls out to admire. Kodomo no Hi, or Boy's Day, in May, is a time when boys participate in carp (Koinobori) kite contests. The Moon Viewing Festival is held when there is a full moon at harvest time, in September. Rice cakes are made as an offering to the moon and dinner is eaten by moonlight.

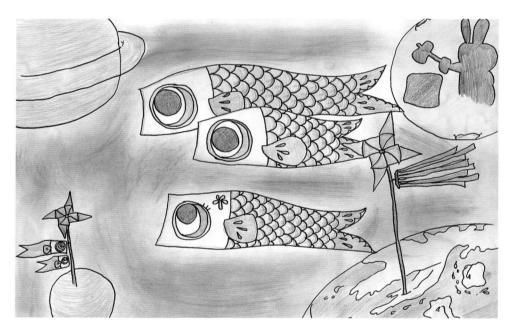

Free Koinobori from Space
Mari Hosotani (age 14)
Can you see the carp kites flying free in space, next to the moon? The Japanese say that if you look closely at a full moon you will see a rabbit making rice cakes. What do you see when you look at a full moon?

Moon Viewing Festival
Ryo Asada (age 8)

In traditional Japanese houses, straw mats, or tatami, are laid on the floors. Because the houses are small, people sleep on the floor on mattresses, called futons, that can be rolled up during the day and stored in cupboards so the room may be used for other purposes. In Japan, as a sign of respect and for cleanliness, you are expected to remove your shoes and put on slippers before entering the house.

Japanese gardens are designed to imitate the real countryside and to bring a sense of perfection, harmony and peace to the viewer from any point they are viewed. For example, a pool in the garden represents a lake, and carefully-placed pebbles take the place of large rocks.

Rice, seaweed, beancurd and vegetables form an important part of the Japanese diet. More fish is eaten here than anywhere else in the world. Sushi – raw fish with rice – is a speciality that has now become popular in many other countries. Japanese people usually eat with a pair of chopsticks, two thin pieces of wood, held in one hand, to pick up the food.

Beckoning cat
Yuka Mori (age 9)
'Welcome to our shop! My name is Maneki-neko. I am a mascot of good fortune. I invite you to enter and spend your money here.'

七福神

Seven Gods of Good Fortune
Eri Veno (age 12)
Can you see Hote, the god of happiness, with his laughing face and big belly?

Hand-painted fans are used with traditional dress, in dance and theatre. Theatre has been a favourite form of entertainment in Japan since ancient times. Two special forms are Noh and Kabuki. Noh, dating back to the 14th century, was inspired by Zen Buddhism and is considered the classical form of theatre. Men play all the roles and there is very little movement. In contrast, Kabuki is a more lively and spectacular performance, with music, dancing and great costumes.

Origami, the art of paper folding, has become part of Japan's cultural heritage. It seems to have originated in China shortly after paper-making began, and was brought to Japan sometime during the sixth century. Gifts were often given in folded paper, which was embellished with a flourish of fancy folds, and this led to the creation of more elaborate and intricate shapes representing animals or objects. Origami cranes are left by visitors at the Sadako monument in the city of Hiroshima as a symbol for all wars to end. Sadako was a young girl who died as a result of the dropping of the Atomic Bomb on Hiroshima towards the end of World War II.

A Kabuki actor delights the audience with stories of heroes carrying out noble deeds. This ivory carving depicts a similar scene.

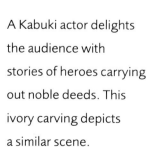

FAR RIGHT: Sadako monument, Hiroshima.

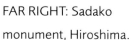

Japanese Brush Painting

Brush painting in Japan is an ancient and honoured art, dating from the 16th century. It takes long years of practice, sometimes up to 15, before a person is ready to paint on their own. The brush stroke is the most important thing about this type of painting. It can show strength and imagination and should always reflect calm, orderly beauty, like nature itself. A simple brush stroke can become a mass of clouds, falling rocks or high peaks.

Music for inspiration

The Art of Japanese Bamboo Flute and Koto by Yamato Ensemble

All the Best from Japan by various artists

Song of the Seashore by James Galway, with the Tokyo String Orchestra

You will need

1 live branch with leaves, possibly bamboo
India ink or black liquid watercolor
2 soft watercolor brushes, 1 large and 1 small
Jar of water
5–10 pieces of white paper (if possible a selection of newsprint, rice paper, tracing or parchment), cut into long strips – say, 22.5cm x 60cm (9in x 24in) or 15cm x 45cm (6in x 18in)
1 long strip of red paper, larger than the white paper
1 wooden rod, stick or bamboo, 25cm (10in)
1 length of black yarn or ribbon, 40cm (16in)
Glue

What to do

1) Hold a brush straight up and down (at right angles to the paper), supported by all four fingers and thumb.

2) Try some brush strokes in the air. Instead of moving your wrist to move the brush, move your arm, from the elbow.

3) Dip your brush in the ink or black watercolor. Wipe it on the side so the tip is pointed.

4) Now try some quick brush strokes on your first piece of paper. Try to imagine what the finished stroke will look like before you make it. In Japan, going over a stroke is not allowed.

5) Study the branch with leaves and try to paint it.

6) Add water to the ink for lighter tones. Do lots of paintings, trying different strokes. Always keep them quick and simple.

7) Allow them to dry.

8) Now choose your favourite painting to glue onto the long piece of red background paper. Fold the top edge over and glue it down. Slip the rod into it and tie yarn at each end for hanging it up.

Ecuador

Ecuador *

You pronounce this:

Eh-kwa-DOOR

*As you can see, the English and Spanish spellings and pronunciation are the same.

Otavalo nestles in the Valley of the Volcanoes.

Ecuador – which means 'straddling the Equator' – is the smallest republic in South America. It is bordered by Colombia and Peru, and is a fascinating country, filled with natural wonders. The snow-capped Andes mountain range, with several active volcanoes, runs the length of the country. To the east you will find the lush rainforests of the Oriente region. The Pacific Ocean lies between the beautiful coastline of the mainland and the rich animal life of the Galápagos Islands.

Pacha Mamá: Our Country Is Rich in Nature
Gabriel Perez (age 10)
Pacha Mamá means Mother Earth in Quichua, the language of the Incas, still spoken by many today. Gabriel's picture shows us many things about life in Ecuador – how many can you see?

An unusual plant from the Ecuadorian rainforest.

Ecuador has a population of 12 million people. Quito, the capital, is a beautiful city, with white-washed houses and red tiled roofs, flanked by mountains. Mount Pichincha, a volcanic mountain west of Quito, erupted in 1999, dropping ash on the city and causing a lot of excitement! Apart from volcanic eruptions, the region also has to contend with frequent earthquakes and the unpredictable weather phenomenon of El Niño.

Some of Quito's many apartment blocks.

Grupo Chayag
Lidia Vega (age 12)

Mountain Life
Carla Davila (age 10)

The native people of Ecuador have ancestors that date back to before the Inca Empire. The remains of a temple to Inti (the sun) – the Inca's supreme deity – can be found at Ingapirca. The official language of Ecuador is Spanish. It was brought to most of South and Central America when the Spanish conquered the region in the 1500s.

Ecuador has rich cultural traditions. The folk music of the Andes has a haunting sound, made with wind and percussion instruments, including the well-known bamboo panpipes and flutes.

The Galápagos Islands are 658 miles (1060km) offshore, along the line of the Equator. They are home to some unique animal and plant life, which, after he visited the islands in the mid-19th century, led Charles Darwin to develop his theory of evolution. As the islands were formed millions of years ago from underwater volcanoes, all the species now found here originally arrived by sea or air, or by hitching a lift on another organism.

Balsa wood carvings made by people on the Galápagos Islands.

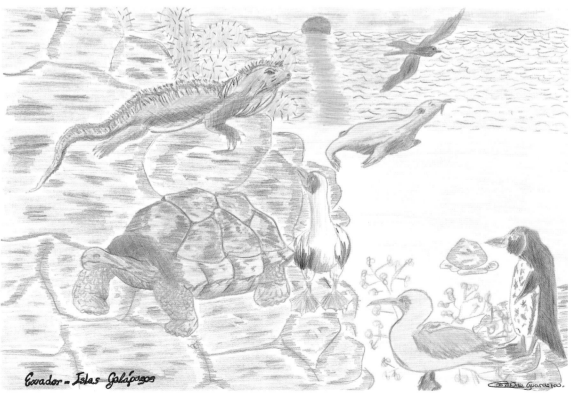

Ecuador - Islas Galápagos

Pan Pipes
Paola Cuyo (age 13)
Do you see the shape on this musician's tunic? His ancestors, the Inca, worshipped a sun god.

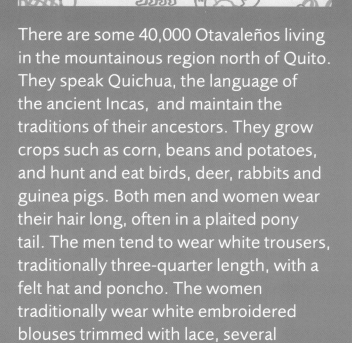

The city of Otavalo's colourful Saturday market, Mercado de Ponchos, sells food and livestock but is most famous for its crafts, including pottery, painting, sculpture, goldsmithing and weaving. Distinctive handmade sweaters are knitted by the local Otavaleño Indians and sold the world over.

There are some 40,000 Otavaleños living in the mountainous region north of Quito. They speak Quichua, the language of the ancient Incas, and maintain the traditions of their ancestors. They grow crops such as corn, beans and potatoes, and hunt and eat birds, deer, rabbits and guinea pigs. Both men and women wear their hair long, often in a plaited pony tail. The men tend to wear white trousers, traditionally three-quarter length, with a felt hat and poncho. The women traditionally wear white embroidered blouses trimmed with lace, several layers of ankle-length skirts, a shawl and several necklaces.

Visiting the Farm
Martin Sebastian Flores
(age 9)

OPPOSITE: *Isla Galápagos*
José Goarderos (age 12)
Can you identify the sea lion, penguin, turtle, iguana, albatross, and blue-footed booby?

Tigua is a village in the high Andes where the people also speak Quichua and live much like their ancestors did. Most are farmers, who grow potatoes and grain, and herd sheep and llamas, but they are also known for their distinctive paintings. Painting on a flat surface is a new art form for them. Before this, they painted decorations on drums and masks for festivals. They began painting on sheepskin stretched on wood frames in the 1970s, and found that the colourful paintings of their traditional way of life were popular with tourists. The carefully painted details show farming or festivals, musicians or ancient stories.

Another unusual art form from Ecuador, mostly made for tourists, is masapan miniatures. These tiny sculptures, made from flour or potato-plaster dough, look a lot like the paintings from Tigua, with lots of colourful detail. They often show a charming and humorous side of life.

You might like to study these paintings and then make up a story to share with your family or friends. Or maybe you'd like to make your own Tigua style painting, telling your own story. BELOW: Decorative work like this lacquerware tray is popular throughout Ecuador.

Ecuadorian Masapan Miniatures

Artists in Ecuador use special potato-plaster dough to form the shapes for their masapan miniatures. When they are dry, they paint them with bright enamel paints. You are sure to enjoy making similar small clay-dough sculptures. It is fun to make the dough and then shape it into all kinds of objects.

Music for inspiration

Listen to some Ecuadorian music. The sounds of panpipes and flutes will help your imagination come up with some great ideas. For example:

Music from the Highlands of South America (Peru, Bolivia, Ecuador) by Markahuasi

En La Cantina by Julio Jaranello and Daniel Santos

Lo Mejor De Ecuador by Julio Jaranello

You will need

1 cup cornflour
2 cups baking soda
1¼ cups water
Bright tempera or acrylic paints
Fine-tipped permanent marker
Small brushes
Glue
Flat piece of cardboard for drying

What to do

1) Combine the cornflour, baking soda and water in a pan. Heat over a medium heat until you have a thick dough. Cool this until you can handle it, then kneed it well until it feels ready to form into shapes. Form the dough into a large ball and keep it covered with plastic until you are ready to use it.

2) Decide what object or scene your masapan sculpture will be. Will you try to make something that looks Ecuadorian or would you like to make something from your own life?

3) Begin by forming the largest shape (boat, truck, basket, etc.) you are going to make. Pinch a small amount of dough off the large ball. Keep the ball covered to keep it soft and moist. Pinch, pull, shape, roll, and press to form the shape you want. When you are happy with the way it looks, carefully set it aside on the cardboard.

4) Carry on pinching off little bits of dough to make all the shapes you want, setting them aside on the cardboard to dry. You might try tiny shapes of fruit, animals, flowers, etc. Have fun!

5) Put your cardboard tray of shapes in a safe, warm, dry place for a few days until your sculptures have dried thoroughly. You can bake them in a warm oven (180°C/350°F/gas mark 4) for 2 hours if you prefer. You want the shapes to dry separately so don't let them touch each other.

6) When completely dry, your shapes are ready to paint. Paint each miniature shape separately. Do you want to paint all the sides, tops and bottoms? You decide. Put the shapes aside to dry as you finish each piece.

7) When the paint is dry, you are ready to assemble the pieces. Try placing them together first and when you are happy with the way it looks, carefully glue each piece in place. You will then have a family treasure to put on a shelf!

Bluebird by the Well
J Pradeep Sudakar (age 9)

India

भारत

Hindi for India. You pronounce this:

PAH-rat

There are many languages and scripts across India including Urdu, Panjabi, and Devanagari in the north; Teluga, Kannada, Tamil and Malayalam in the south; Bengali and Oriya in the east and Gujarati in the west. The official language is Hindi, which is taught in schools along with English, and is spoken in most of the country.

ભારત

Gujarati for India

ਭਾਰਤ

Panjabi for India

ভারত

Bengali for India

These children live in the southern city of Chennai (also known as Madras).

India is a magical and colourful place. There are more people living here than in any other country in the world except China, more people than in the continents of Europe and North America combined. At least a quarter of the 1 billion population lives in towns or cities. Dehli is the capital but the largest cities are Mumbai (also known as Bombay) and Calcutta. The landscape is varied, from the high snow-capped Himalayas in the north (where the great Ganges, or Ganga, River begins) to the fertile plains of the Ganga delta, the deserts of Rajasthan, and the Western and Eastern Ghat Mountains overlooking the Arabian Sea and the Bay of Bengal.

Children at the Dalit Liberation Education Trust making pictures – you can see two of their works of art opposite.

LEFT: The Taj Mahal.

RIGHT: A poster of Mahatma ('the great soul') Gandhi adorns the Old Fort, Dehli.

The Mogul Emperor Shah Jahan built the Taj Mahal (pictured opposite) in Agra in 1648 as a tomb for his beloved wife, Mumtaz Mahal. The Taj is built of white marble and is considered by many to be the most beautiful building in the world.

Mahatma Gandhi is one of India's greatest heroes. His campaign of peaceful protests, called satyagrah, led to India's independence from Britain in 1947. He is also responsible for the outlawing of the caste system that automatically placed people in different occupations because of the group in which they were born. Even today, however, the lowest caste, the Dalit (or Untouchables), still face discrimination.

Cut Paper City
V Balu (age 8)

Rural Fishing Scene
S Sathiya (age 12)

Many people in rural villages live in houses made of mud and straw with thatched roofs. Cow dung is dried to use as fuel for cooking, which is generally done in clay pots. Indian meals are usually served with rice, or a flat bread pancake called chapati. Lentils, or dal, and vegetable curry cooked with a variety of spices, are common dishes. Rural homes have little furniture and people often sit on the floor to eat. Some villages have wells and pumps for water. Farming outside the village is hard work. Although some villages have tractors, animals – frequently oxen – help pull the carts.

Most Indian women continue to wear the traditional dress called a sari, pictured on this page. A sari is a very long piece of brightly-coloured cloth, wrapped around the body in a particular way. Many Hindu women paint a red dot, called a tika, on their foreheads on religious occasions. At other times this decorative mark is called a bindi. A traditional dress for men is a dhoti, which is similar to a sari.

Bhuratanatyam (Classical Dancer)
Minal Desai (age14)

Shepherdess with Baby and Sheep
Ashkay Gupta (age 14)

More than 80% of the people in India are Hindus. There are also a significant number of Muslims amd a smaller number of Christians, Sikhs, Buddhists and Jains. Hinduism is characterised by the worship of many gods, each of which is responsible for some aspect of life. Most Hindus believe in one Supreme Being, Brahma, the creator of the universe.

RIGHT: Miniature elephant sculpture.

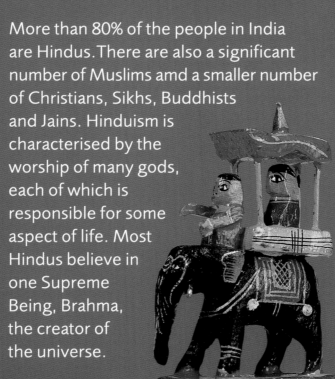

Many Hindus see three gods as all-powerful: Brahma (Creator), Vishnu (Preserver) and Shiva (Destroyer). Krishna is one of the most popular gods. He is an incarnation of Vishnu, and has a human face often portrayed with blue skin. Ganesh (the elephant god) is another favourite. Meetings and special family gatherings often begin with prayers to Ganesh, the protector and a remover of obstacles. Representations of these and other gods can be seen everywhere, in statues, temple carvings, posters and postcards.

Honouring the Cow
Anushka Gupta (age 9)

The ancient city of Varanasi, the City of Light, was built beside the sacred Ganges River. Indians call the river Ganga Mai, or Mother Ganges. Many holy temples were built beside the river, and people come to bathe there, believing it will wash away their sins. Varanasi is also a centre for handicrafts, such as silks and embroidery, ornamental brasswork and glass beads, which are exported worldwide.

The tradition of Abhala, or mirror work, began in the desert of western India where a natural source of reflective mica was found. The tiny mirrors, which are secured in place by a variety of interesting embroidery stitches, reflect any light in dark interiors in a magical way. The designs suggest something from nature or depict details from a beloved story. This Abhala hanging was made in Kashmir and its patchwork design represents the local terrain – fields, crops, water and wells.

Children light candles during Diwali.

Happy Diwali
Kruti J Desai (age 10)
The Festival of Light, Diwali, is believed by some to have begun in ancient times when the beloved epic hero, Rama, was welcomed home after 14 years of battle, during which he saved his wife from a terrible monster. To help him find his way home, people decorated their doorways, lit lanterns and set off firecrackers to ward off any evil monsters who might be about.

Cut Paper Alpanas

Alpanas began with women making a decoration at the entrance to their homes by mixing flour and coloured powder, then dripping it through their fingers. This made a welcoming design of curving, flowing shapes on the ground. Paper alpanas are cut paper designs that are hung in doorways to help celebrate the festival of Diwali. They are made by cutting folded paper so that a balanced pattern results when the paper is unfolded.

Music for inspiration

Maharishi Gandharva Veda Music/Rain Melody by Amar Nath on Bamboo Flute

Dhola Maru by the Musafir Ensembe

The Sounds of India by Ravi Shankar

You will need

Bright coloured photocopier paper (or similar), 21cm x 30cm (8½in x 11in)
Light brown children's art paper, 23cm x 32cm (9in x 12in)
Pencil
Scissors
Glue
Glitter for decoration

What to do:

1) Fold the copy paper into quarters – in half and then in half again.

2) With a pencil, draw a design, keeping in mind the folds, the centre and the edges.

3) Cut carefully so that your scissors cut the four layers and the design is left intact on the folds.

4) Unfold your cut paper and enjoy the repeated and balanced design. Fold it up again if you want to try a bit more cutting. You can try to poke into some of the shapes to open up 'windows' in your design. Notice how the positive and negative shapes work together for a complete design.

5) When you are happy with the design, glue it onto the brown paper or simply hang it in your doorway as a welcoming decoration. Add some glitter, if you like, for extra fancy alpanas. Try stringing a number of them together as a decoration for special occasions, such as Diwali in October/November.

Russia
Россия

You pronounce this:
Ra-ssee-YAH

The word 'grand' describes Russia in many ways. In area, it is by far the largest country in the world, spanning parts of two continents, Europe and Asia. It has the largest lake, the Caspian Sea, which is actually a salt lake. On its eastern shore, Russia has the longest continuous coastline of any country in the world. Then there is the incredible scenery, varying from flat, swampy marshland to rolling hills; from rivers and deep canyons to complex mountain systems with volcanoes. Russia has grand seasons too. There are long, cold winters and short, cool summers. In Siberia, the most northern part of the country, winter temperatures average minus 60°C (minus 76°F).

Portrait of My Friend
Lena Martynyuk (age11)

The children who made these pictures live in the town of Staraya Russa, a mineral spring resort that boasts the biggest natural fountain of mineral water in Europe. Many folkloric traditions continue to be observed here, such as decorated eggs in spring and yule logs at the winter solstice, which date back to ancient times. Throughout the year, there are festivals, including a wonderful celebration in March to welcome spring, when children shout and run to the fields, scattering bread for the birds.

Four-fifths of the 150-milllion population live in European Russia – that is, west of the Ural Mountains – in and around the capital, Moscow, and St Petersburg. Moscow's Cathedral of St Basil is very distinctive, with its eight towers and colourful onion-shaped cupolas. It sits at one end of Red Square. On the opposite side of the square are the ancient walls of the Kremlin, which surround the government buildings.

Fun on the Bridge
Dima Filin (age 11)

Urban housing, Moscow.

Many of Moscow's inhabitants live in apartment blocks. In some of these buildings there is only one kitchen, which is shared by a number of apartments. In the countryside, traditional single-storey wooden cottages, or izba, are still common. They resemble the houses illustrated in old fairy tales – and in Oleg's painting below.

Russian people grow much of their own food, whether it is in a communal garden in the city or a field in the country.

Because Russia is so far north and the growing season is short, there are limited fruits and vegetables available. Soup is a common dish, with borscht being the most famous and delicious recipe. It is made from beetroot, cabbage, and potatoes, and is served hot with sour cream. Russian people always use wooden spoons to eat their soup because, unlike metal, wood doesn't get hot. Very smart!

Traditional wooden cottage.

Motorbikes by a Country House
Oleg Mateev (age 10)

The game of chess was introduced to Russia by Arab traders in the eighth century, 100 years before it reached Western Europe. Not confined to the nobility as it was in other countries, chess was immediately popular with all classes, and this is still the case today. Perhaps

this is why many of the greatest players in history, such as Anatoly Karpov and Gary Kasparov (the youngest-ever world champion in 1985 at the age of 22), have come from Russia.

Most traditional Russian homes have hot tea available, for family and visitors, at any time of day. The tea is served from a samovar (meaning boiling pot), which is an urn, usually of copper, with a separate central cylinder where hot coals are placed. The hot coals heat the water and tea leaves, and keep the drink hot. The tea is served in glasses, sometimes in holders with metal handles.

ABOVE: *Deep into Winter*
Shmelev Nickolai (age 14)
RIGHT: *Lena Holding her Special Book*
Nadya Knyazeva (age 15)

There is a long tradition in Russia of crafting beautiful eggs, sometimes as jewellery, or as paintings or designs. The symbolic importance of eggs dates back to ancient times, when they represented new beginnings and even the earth itself. In 1884, Karl Fabergé designed a jewelled egg for the Russian Imperial Family. This became a yearly tradition and Fabergé eggs are now highly-desirable treasures the world over.

Nesting dolls or Matryoshka – meaning grandmother – are popular the world over as an example of Russian folk art and as a toy. Each doll in a set is the same shape and usually the same design, but the sizes change, getting smaller and smaller so they can fit one inside the other. A set can symbolise generations of women in the same family.

A Fabergé egg decorated with rubies, aquamarines and diamonds.

A set of Matryoshka nesting dolls.

Papier-mâché items are often lacquered and painted with images from nature or a scene from a favourite Russian folk or fairy tale. Here is one that tells the story of The Stone Flower:

There once lived a master stone cutter. A young boy became his beloved and talented apprentice. They were like father and son. When the boy grew to be a handsome young man he fell in love and married. One day a local lord ordered a stone cup to be made for the Tzar. The young man wanted to make it in the shape of a stone flower. He was unhappy with the results and went off to find the Mistress of Copper Mountain who, he was told, could help him. He found her in a cavern filled with the most amazing jewelled flowers. The mistress fell in love with him and forced him to stay with her. Meanwhile, his beloved wife came in search of her husband. When she found him in the cavern and expressed her grief and love, the Mistress of the Mountain was moved to release them both. She sent them home with the most exquisite box filled with precious jewels. They lived happily ever after and he became the best stone flower carver in the land.

A Matryoshka
Bichkova Tanya (age 13)

Бычкова Таня

Paper Russian Matryoshka design

What better way to learn to count? You carry around one toy, then open it up and have seven or more to play with, imagining they are a family, or a group of friends. In this art activity we will use the idea of repeat patterns and different sizes to make our own decorative design that reflects this special Russian art.

Music for inspiration

Russian Folk Dances by Moiseyer Dance Company

Russian Favourite Music by Ossipov Balalaika Orchestra

Best of Russian Folk Songs by Balalaika Ensembe Wolga

What you need

1 sheet of light-coloured children's art paper or photocopy paper, 30cm x 42cm (12in x 18in)
1 sheet of black or dark-coloured children's art paper, 30cm x 42cm (12in x 18in)
Scissors
Pencil
Black permanent marker pen
Tools to decorate – coloured marker pens, thick and thin; crayons; oil pastels; tempera paint; and metallic paint marker
Glue

What to do

1) Fold the light-coloured paper in half, then again, and then a third time so that you end up with eight equal sections when it is opened.

2) With the paper folded, draw a Matryoshka shape with the pencil. This should be very simple, just a slight curve at the shoulders, rounded at the head and straight at the feet.

3) Carefully cut around your shape, through all the folded paper, so you end up with eight identical shapes.

4) Now cut around each shape so that it becomes smaller than the one before it.

5) Begin decorating the largest shape. Draw a circle for the face, then add the features. Draw other outlines – perhaps feet and hands – to decorate the entire shape. Use your imagination or get some ideas from the Matryoshka pictured here. Now fill in with colour, using one or more of the listed tools, and add bits of metallic paint marker for accent.

6) When you are pleased with the way your largest Matryoshka looks, copy its pattern onto the other shapes, or change it slightly as you go.

7) When you are finished and the shapes are dry, arrange them on the dark background paper. Try different ways. Do you like them in a line or do you like them turned other ways? Arrange them any way you like. When you are happy with your design, carefully glue them to the paper.

8) If you choose, you can complete your design by painting or drawing a border, or adding other areas of interest.

Hanging Clothes
Hülya Ağca (age 9)

Turkey

Türkiye

You pronounce this:
Tewr-KEEYE

The medieval fortress at Alanya is enclosed by a 6km (3³/₄ mile) wall.

The art on these pages was made by children from an orphanage in Istanbul.

If you lived in Turkey you would never be very far from the sea. The country is bordered on three sides by water: the Black Sea to the north, the Mediterranean to the south and the Aegean to the west. There are 159 islands, most uninhabited. A narrow strip of water, the Bosporus Strait, cuts Turkey in two. Two great bridges have been built here, connecting the European part, Thrace, to the much larger Asian part, Anatolia. Eastern Turkey is particularly mountainous. The highest peak is Mount Ararat, where some say Noah's ark landed after the flood.

Life by the Water
Eren Yavuzer (age 12)

Street traders sell fresh fish caught that day.

Istanbul is Turkey's largest city. It is a busy port, with ferries and cargo ships that pass through the Bosporus on their way north to the Black Sea and the countries of Georgia, Russia, Ukraine, Romania and Bulgaria. If you took a walk in Istanbul you would see crowds of people, street traders, big buildings, small shops, many mosques, bridges and boats. You might walk by a coffee-house where people meet to play cards, chat and drink coffee made by grinding the coffee beans into powder and boiling it in water with sugar.

Fishing on the Bosporus
Tuna Alkan (age 9)
Tuna's drawing shows us some of the different kinds of fish found in the waters around Istanbul and sold by the street sellers like the one in the photograph above. Where do you think your fish for supper comes from?

A brass shop in the Grand Bazaar, Istanbul, full of shiny pots and trays.

The Grand Bazaar in Istanbul is enclosed by eight iron gates, and is an amazing labyrinth of over 4,000 shops. Many Turkish crafts are on sale here, to local people and tourists alike – from carpets to leather and suede accessories; and from ceramics to brass and alabaster ornaments. The hand-woven carpets, made from silk, wool or cotton, are more like works of art than something functional to step on. These kilims have repeated motifs that are particular to a region but the designs are an artistic expression of the weaver.

Examples of the beautifully-crafted carpets and ceramics produced by Turkish artisans.

Traditional Turkish Dancer
Duygu Tunç (age 9)
Duygu's portrait is made with all kinds of materials, many of which can be found in the pazar (bazaar).

OPPOSITE: *Night Drummer*
Direnç Albayrak (age 7)
During Ramadan, drummers alert the people to get up and eat breakfast before the time of fasting begins.

Tiles from the Blue
Mosque, Istanbul.

Most of the people in Turkey are Muslim. They visit mosques like this one, Süleymaniye, to worship, meet, teach and study. The Turkish word for mosque is cami, meaning 'a place where people gather' in Arabic. Süleymaniye displays a cascade of domes on the outside and 138 arched windows that transform the inside of the mosque into an inspiring space of colour and light. Beautiful prayer carpets line the floors and ceramic tiles, of calligraphy or flowing design, decorate the walls and ceiling.

The Süleymaniye
Mosque, Istanbul.

It is traditional for girls, especially in rural places, to prepare oya (handmade lace, like the example pictured here), needlework and embroidery, from an early age. These items are set aside, to be used in their future married lives.

An artist in Turkey is called a sanatkar or sanatçi. True works of art must communicate both emek, the necessary labour and energy, and sanat, the spirit of the artist.

Miniature paintings date back to the 14th century in Persia and even earlier in India. In Turkey, artists created miniature paintings as a record of courtly and military life. They tell of an inspiring world, as it should be. It might be a religious, historical or mythical tale, or simply an episode from daily life. The painting below depicts the tale of the Know-It-All Turban:

An illiterate man [the one on the left] *receives a letter and asks Hodja, a teacher, to read it for him. Hodja tries but can't make it out, probably because the letter was written in Arabic or Persian, not Turkish. 'I can't read it,' he confesses. 'Have someone else read it.' The man gets angry: 'You are supposed to be a learned man, a teacher. You ought to be ashamed of the turban you're wearing.' Hodja takes his turban off, puts it on the man's head, and says: 'If you think the turban knows it all, see if you can read the letter!'*

Miniature paintings often tell of heroes and friends joining forces against evil demons. They might appear on the pages of antique books to illustrate the writing, or even on ceramic pieces, like this pitcher.

Turkish miniature painting

The traditional Turkish art of miniature painting sets out to tell a story. The paintings often combine words and pictures and become a kind of 'visual poetry'. They are usually presented with beautifully decorative multiple borders and are embellished with gold paint.

Music for inspiration

Sufi Music of Turkey by Kudsi Erguner, Süleyman Erguner

Musique Persian by Pierre Toureille

You will need

1 sheet of white drawing paper, approx. 21cm x 30cm (9in x 12in)
1 sheet of black children's art paper, approx. 24cm x 33cm (10in x 13in)
1 sheet of coloured children's art paper, approx. 30cm x 39cm (12in x 15in)
2 strips of decorated paper (wallpaper or gift wrap), approx. 27cm x 4cm (11in x 1½in)
2 strips of decorated paper (wallpaper or gift wrap), approx. 36cm x 4cm (14in x 1½in)
1 thin black permanent marker pen
Variety of coloured markers, thick and thin
Watercolour paints
1 gold paint marker
Glue

What to do

1) Using the thin black marker pen, make a line drawing that tells a story – perhaps a tale from a book (such as King Arthur or a story from A Thousand and One Nights) or a special tradition or celebration (maybe a wedding or Harvest Festival). Or perhaps you could draw a scene from the Know-It-All Turban (see opposite). Make sure you include lots of details as you draw, like where your story takes place, the season and all of the characters.

2) When you have finished your drawing, fill it in with colour, using coloured marker pens and/or watercolour paints. Let it dry for a few minutes.

3) Glue your picture to the black paper so that you have an even border around the edges. Then glue this to the larger coloured paper, again making sure it is centred.

4) Take the strips of decorated paper and glue them carefully in the space between the black border and the coloured frame, so they meet neatly at the corners.

5) Finish your picture by using the gold pen to accent both the picture and the frame. Outline parts of your story and add small details like lines or dots. Your miniature painting should look very decorative when you are finished.

Kenya

Kenya*

Swahili for Kenya. You pronounce this:
KEN-yaw

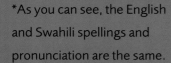

*As you can see, the English and Swahili spellings and pronunciation are the same.

Kenya , which straddles the northern and southern hemispheres, has very distinct land areas. The Great Rift Valley, a deep crack in the earth, runs the length of the country. There are stunning views from its steep cliffs, including shimmering soda lakes teeming with flamingos. Mount Kenya, Africa's second highest mountain, is part of the Highland area to the east. This is the most fertile part of Kenya, and the extra rainfall and good soil make it ideal for growing tea and coffee. The north of the country, bordered by Sudan and Ethiopia, is dry desert. To the west is Uganda and the fertile shores of Lake Victoria. Further south is the grassy savannah with its thorn trees, which is mainly used for grazing cattle. And to the east are the beautiful warm waters of the Indian Ocean.

Arches resembling crossed tusks form the gateway to Mombasa.

The children who created these paintings live in the bustling city of Mombasa, Kenya's chief sea port, on the coast of the Indian Ocean. From here, goods such as cotton, sugar and fruits are exported.

The gateway to the city is made to represent the great tusks of the African elephant, so familiar in the countryside of Kenya. The children's pictures tell of warm days and plentiful crops. However, here and throughout Kenya, there is always the real threat that the monsoon rains will not come, leading to drought and failed harvests.

The capital, Nairobi, once a watering hole for the Masai and their cattle, is now a cosmopolitan city of 3.5 million people. The name comes from the Masai words enkare nyarobe meaning sweet water.

Although it is located across the border in Tanzania, the snow-topped Mount Kilimanjaro – the highest peak in Africa – is clearly visible from southern Kenya.

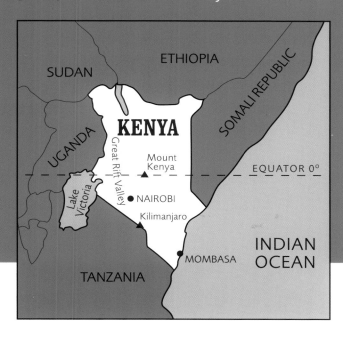

Village by the Sea
Resiba Mlongo (age 15)

Shields and beaded necklaces are made by the Masai for sale at the marketplace.

There are many ethnic groups in Kenya. The largest of these is the Kikuyu which makes up 21% of the 29 million population. They live primarily around Mount Kenya and the fertile lands near Nairobi. They are farmers and have adapted well to the modern world by growing tea and coffee for export. They traditionally live in roundhouses with thatched roofs, and have small gardens.

The Masai are probably the best known ethnic group, although they only make up 2% of the population. They are nomadic herders who travel on foot in search of food for their goats, sheep and cows. Their main food is milk, which is supplemented by blood taken from their cattle. At the age of 16, the men become warriors. They carry long spears, plait their hair and paint their bodies with ochre. They wear plugs in their ears and wrap themselves in distinctive red cloaks. The women shave their heads. Both sexes wear beautiful beaded necklaces and large earrings.

Mother Pounding Grain
Ally Ahmed Sved (age 14)

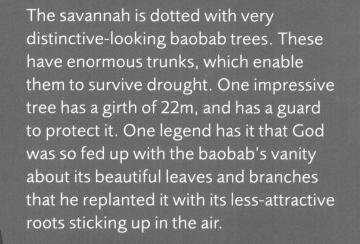

Many visitors to Kenya go on safari. This involves a trip through a national park or game reserve, usually by jeep, with a local guide. If you are lucky you might see the 'Big 5' – lion, leopard, buffalo, elephant and rhino – as well zebra, giraffe, hippo and many species of monkey. Another big attraction for visitors is Kenya's coastline, with its miles of beautiful white sand.

The savannah is dotted with very distinctive-looking baobab trees. These have enormous trunks, which enable them to survive drought. One impressive tree has a girth of 22m, and has a guard to protect it. One legend has it that God was so fed up with the baobab's vanity about its beautiful leaves and branches that he replanted it with its less-attractive roots sticking up in the air.

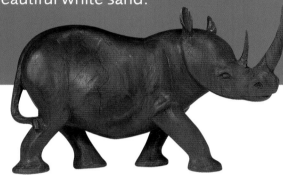

African Patterns
Elves Barraza (age 6)
Why might Elves' picture make you think of dancing and drum music?

Corn Harvest
Jane Mwikali (age 13)

Folk art in Kenya reflects nature and its resources. The colours may come from the different kinds of clay found in the earth, or from plants such as indigo that gives the vibrant blue of the tie-dye bag below. Repeat patterns and designs seem to dance through the art, whether it is on cloth, bowls, faces or walls. We see lines, zig-zags, dots and circles, spirals, triangles and diagonals. The designs often represent shapes from nature like suns, moons, leaves, trees and animals.

Ebony carvings and masks are an important part of African rituals and ceremonies.

TOP RIGHT: The animal necklace is made of carved wood and strung with local dried seeds.

The toy you see below was hand-made by a Kenyan child. It is made from pieces of wood, feathers, rock and string. The head and tail of the bird are attached separately and the string drops through a hole in the wood where the bird stands. When held by the end and moved, the head and tail bob up and down. Why not try to make something similar yourself!

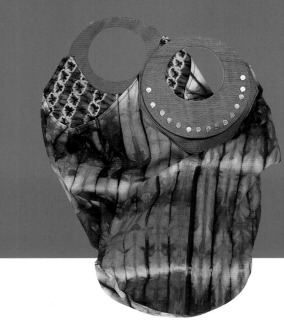

Village Work and Play
Oketch Baraka (age 8)

Kenyan Camel Bag with Traditional Design

Camel bags – usually made of leather – have been used for centuries in parts of Africa and the Middle East. Occasionally, little children have been known to have a good sleep in them. Here, we are creating a smaller version out of paper. Think about nature's shapes and let the music, with its drumming sounds, help you design a pattern for your bag, full of rhythm and repetition.

Music for inspiration

African music will help inspire and enhance the activity. For example:

The Rough Guide to the Music of Kenya and Tanzania by various artists

Kenya Dance Mania by Earthworks

Africa by Miriam Makeba

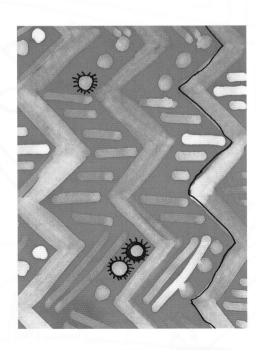

You will need

1 sheet earth-tone children's art paper, 30.5cm x 45cm (12in x 18in)
Small amount of watered-down bleach (1 part water to 1 part bleach)
Cotton buds
Marker pens (black, brown, orange, dark red)
Stapler
Scissors

What to do

1) Fold your paper evenly any way you like, pressing hard on the creases.

2) Now unfold the paper. The folds will form the basis of your design.

3) Carefully dip a cotton bud into the watered-down bleach and draw it along the folds. Then add repeat patterns and lines to fill the paper. Dots also work well.

4) The design will quickly reveal itself as it bleaches the paper. When you are happy with the design, leave it dry.

5) Add colour with your marker pens, outlining, colouring in, whatever takes your fancy!

6) Create your bag by folding the paper in half lengthways. Cut a 2.5cm (1in) strip off the top. Staple the sides and bottom, leaving 4cm (1½in) at the bottom so you can cut a fringe. Staple the strip to the corners of the open top to make a strap.

Pine Forest by the Lake
Max Van Tilburg (age 8)

USA

Oh sto ron non ke

Mowhawk for USA. You pronounce this:

oh stow loon nuh gay

The children who made this artwork live in the northeastern part of the US. They experience four very different seasons each year: in summer they enjoy baseball and vacation time; in autumn (fall) there is school and harvest time; in winter there is fun in the snow, hockey and holiday time; and in spring warm temperatures return, waterfalls roar and trees burst into bloom.

The United States of America is a vast, scenic country made up of 50 states. It stretches from Alaska and the pack ice of the Arctic Ocean in the north, to Florida and the tropical waters of the Gulf of Mexico in the south. One of its states, the volcanic islands of Hawaii, is 2,000 miles off the west coast, in the Pacific Ocean. The population of around 270 million includes the Native American peoples whose ancestors were living there when Europeans first arrived about 500 years ago. People from all over the globe have come to the US, some originally in slavery, others for its promise of freedom and the hope of work and a comfortable way of life.

Ready for Hockey
Jamie Mark (age 10)

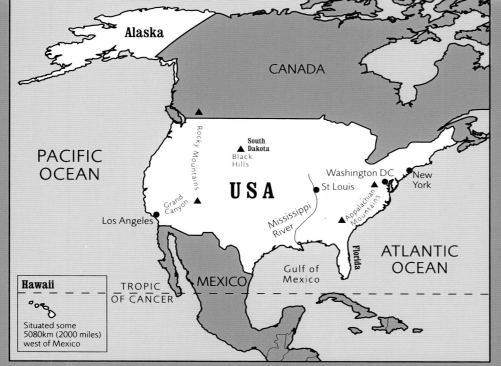

If you travelled west from New York on the Atlantic coast to Los Angeles on the Pacific coast, it would take you several days. You would first cross the forested Appalachian Mountains, then travel through the flat farmland of the Mid-West – the 'breadbasket' of the country – with fields of wheat as far as the eye can see. You would cross the Mississippi River at St Louis before encountering the dry, grassy Great Plains where awesome herds of bison once roamed. Finally, you would have a steep climb over the Rocky Mountains, maybe taking a detour to the amazing Grand Canyon, before descending to the arid desert of Death Valley and on to Los Angeles, the home of Hollywood.

OPPOSITE TOP: The Grand Canyon, Arizona.
RIGHT: New York City; Pumpkin patch.

Sail on the Lake
Yann Schutter (age 12)

Harvest Still Life
Lauren Skye (age 14)

BELOW: New York apartment blocks; a mural celebrates ethnic diversity.

Washington DC is the capital of the United States, but New York – with nearly 8 million inhabitants – is the largest city. It is a really exciting place to visit or to live. The world famous Statue of Liberty (left) stands in the city's harbour and welcomes people approaching by boat. Central Park, a large oasis of green in the middle of the city, is a favourite place for children and joggers.

Most people in New York City live in tall apartment buildings. There's little need to own a car here as underground trains – subways – take you almost anywhere you need to go. There are different neighbourhoods in the city, places where Italian, Greek, Irish, Jamaican, Ecuadorian, Chinese and Vietnamese people, as well as many other groups, live. Here, you can eat the traditional food of these countries; and you can see people in their native costumes, speaking their native language. You can also help celebrate the national holidays of their native countries.

Grandma's House
Spencer Barnes (age 7)

The 60ft-high heads of four American presidents – George Washington, Thomas Jefferson, Theodore Roosevelt and Abraham Lincoln – are carved in the rock of Mount Rushmore, in the Black Hills of South Dakota. Nearby at Thunderhead Mountain is the even bigger, athough still incomplete, carving of Sioux warrior Crazy Horse on horseback.

A favourite public holiday in the US is Thanksgiving, which is held in November. This is a great family feast – usually of roast turkey – to honour the Native Americans who helped the Pilgrims, the first English settlers, to make America their new home. Another major holiday is the 4th of July, also called Independence Day, which celebrates when the American colonies declared their independence from Great Britain in 1776. It is always celebrated with fireworks and picnics, and children love to be taken to amusement parks, where they can go on all kinds of wild and exciting rides.

Fourth of July Celebration
Marcus Bullen (age 9)

Amusement Park
Theo Bogin (age 7)

The Iroquois, or Haudenosaunee (People of the Longhouse), are Native Americans who have lived in the northeast since before American independence. They still honour their traditions, which emphasise a life dedicated to gaining respect, peace and gentle harmony. On special occasions they wear buckskin and feather hats and perform native music and dances. They teach their children to make native crafts, mostly from things found in nature.

ABOVE AND RIGHT:
Replica Hiawatha wampum belt and traditional knife sheath by Jacob Conners (age 11).

BELOW: Traditional Iroquois pouches made by Jacob Conners (age 11) and Will Conners (age 14).

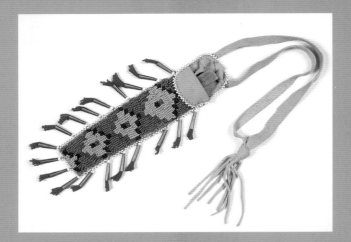

The US has a great tradition of patchwork design, ever since the time of the early English and Dutch settlers. It was originally considered an economical way of using up scraps of fabric, stitching them together to make something larger, often a bed quilt. The patches were always placed in creative ways, using colour, shapes and texture to make beautiful and original pieces of patterned art. Some quilt designs have fascinating names, like Slave Chain and Indian Trail. Some names are descriptive, like Windmill, which is a design of triangles joined at a point, or Milky Way, a grouping of large and small stars. A popular design, the Crazy Quilt, is a random pattern that makes use of scraps of all shapes, sizes and colours, sometimes finished with metallic embroidery and fancy buttons or pearls.

RIGHT: American quilt designs.

Patchwork quilt design

The basic shapes used in patchwork are geometric – including squares, triangles, diamonds and rectangles. The straight sides of these shapes make it easy to connect them together in a solid design. We are going to use paper to recreate the effect, but for even more fun, you could try this project using fabric scraps and fabric glue!

Music for inspiration

Play some traditional US music. Here are two very different types:

Appalachian Journey by Ma, Meyer, O'Connor etc, songs by Stephen Foster et al

Any performance by Preservation Hall Jazz Band, New Orleans

You will need

1 large square piece of coloured children's art paper, 30cm x 30cm (12in x 12in) or larger
2 or more pieces of other paper, half the size of the first piece (these can be solid colours or patterned – like origami or wrapping paper – or you could make your own pattern with coloured marker pens on a plain piece of paper)
Scissors
Glue
Gold and silver paint markers, with fine point
Sequins and small flat buttons

What to do

1) Decide on what kind of quilt design you want to make and what kind of geometric shapes you need to cut for it. You might want to try one of the ones pictured here, make up your own, or try a Crazy Quilt pattern.

2) Using the smaller papers, cut out the geometric shapes you have decided upon. If you are using squares, rectangles or triangles you might try creasing the paper before you cut it. You can also use the shape(s) you want to repeat as a template by tracing it on folded paper and then cutting them out.

3) After you have cut all the shapes, begin laying them in a pattern on the large square. If needed, cut more shapes or trim the ones you have so there is a good fit. When you are happy with the way it looks, carefully glue the pieces on.

4) You might want to finish your patchwork design with some fancy embroidery-like lines, using gold and silver paint markers and maybe adding some sequins or buttons to make it fancy.

Vietnam

Việt Nam

You pronounce this word:
VEE et NAHM

The children who drew these pictures attend a school for the deaf in Ho Chi Minh City

Vietnamese people describe the shape of their country as a bamboo pole with baskets of rice at each end. At its narrowest, Vietnam is only 50km (20 miles) wide. The coastline of this long thin country borders the South China Sea. Vietnam takes its name from the Chinese, meaning 'land to the south'. The longest river in Southeast Asia – the Mekong – runs through the south of the country, and the Red River is found in the north; both flow into large, fertile deltas. Vietnam was once completely covered by dense forest but due to wars and agriculture, more than 70% of the land is now treeless. Today, it has become a custom to plant trees in springtime, and children learn about planting and taking care of trees at school.

Ho Chi Minh City covers a vast sprawling area, which stretches from the South China Sea almost to the Cambodian border.

After a long history of invasion, Vietnam is now a country at peace. It has a population of 80 million, mainly occupying the lowland and coastal areas. The largest and busiest city is Ho Chi Minh City (formerly called Saigon) in the south but the capital is Hanoi in the north. The country values education and is proud of its 88% literacy rate.

Religion in Vietnam is a variety of Buddhism, Confucianism, Taoism and Animism. People worship their ancestors and most have small shrines in their homes to honour family members who have died. At prayer times, near the temples, you might hear drums, bells and gongs sounding. The Lion-Dog is a favourite mythological creature, and statues like the one above are often placed as a guard at entrances.

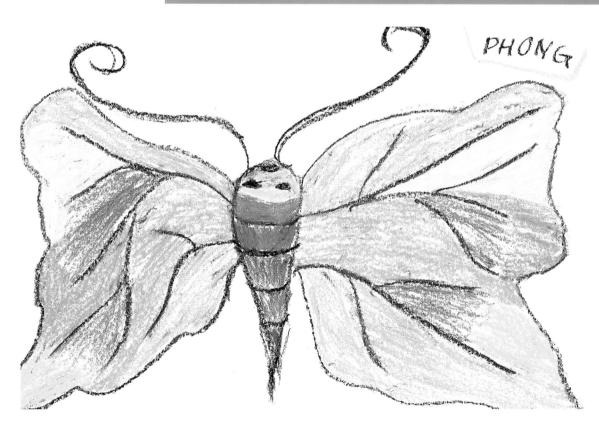

PHONG

My Rainbow Butterfly
Phong (age 10)

A Vietnamese Buddha, with a thousand arms and a thousand eyes.

The weather, especially in the southern part of the country, is often hot and humid so dress is usually comfortable, in the form of trousers and tunics. Schoolgirls dress in an all-white version of this traditional dress, called Ao Dai. Cone-shaped hats are often worn as well.

Cyclos can be hailed along most city streets. These are three-wheeled rickshaws, operated by pedal-power, with a seat for the passenger on the front. Cyclos, bicycles and motor bikes are the best way to get around the busy city.

People in Vietnam enjoy many festivals and celebrations. Their favourite is Tet, which is the Vietnamese New Year. Everyone in the country celebrates his or her birthday on this day. It is a time to pay all debts and begin anew. Children believe that dragons (a traditional Vietnamese symbol representing power and nobility, which stands for the country itself) wander the earth during Tet.

Village Visit
Nhựt (age 14)
Notice the similarity between the house that Nhựt has drawn and the houses in the moonlit lacquerware scene above.

People in Vietnam are hardworking, resilient, gracious and optimistic. Many people experience poverty and the older children must work to help their families.

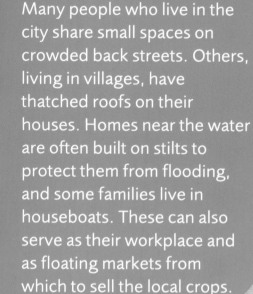

Many people who live in the city share small spaces on crowded back streets. Others, living in villages, have thatched roofs on their houses. Homes near the water are often built on stilts to protect them from flooding, and some families live in houseboats. These can also serve as their workplace and as floating markets from which to sell the local crops.

Many kinds of wonderful and exotic fruits grow in Vietnam, like the dragon fruit (which is purple on the outside with black seeds on the inside), papaya, banana and star fruit (which makes star shapes when cut in slices).

Our New House in
Ho Chi Minh City
Dương (age 10)
This house is built in a modern style but most homes in Vietnam look like those in Nhựt and Căn nhà eá's drawings.

Mekong Delta Farmhouse
Căn nhà eá (age 14)

ABOVE RIGHT: A red dragon water puppet.
BELOW: A lacquerware unicorn water puppet, representing intelligence and goodness.

Vietnamese theatre combines music, singing, recitation, dance and mime. Puppetry is very popular. Water puppetry is a uniquely Vietnamese art form. It is thought to have developed centuries ago in the Red River Delta, when puppeteers were determined to carry on with their show despite a flood. Today this artform, where puppeteers stand waist deep in water behind the set and manipulate puppets with bamboo poles, is considered a national treasure.

There are many traditional Vietnamese folk arts and crafts. Different villages and ethnic groups have their own specialities, like weaving, basketry, carving, printmaking and lacquerware. The art of making lacquerware came to Vietnam in the mid-15th century from China. Before then, the black shiny lacquer was only used for practical purposes like waterproofing boats. The decoration on lacquerware tends to be traditional pictures of scenery, water, birds, fish houses and people. It may tell a story, like 'The Flute Player and the Water Buffalo' below (which is also seen represented in the two traditional crafts below).

BELOW: White cranes painted on a folding lacquerware screen.

RIGHT: Woodblock print on rice paper and lacquerware statue, both representing the story of 'The Flute Player and Water Buffalo'.

Vietnamese Lacquerware Pictures

Lacquer is a creamy white resin tapped from the cay son tree. It is mixed with another resin in an iron container for 40 hours so that it turns black and shiny. Pieces of wood are coated with many layers of this lacquer and then decorated by painting or carving out shapes and inserting pieces of Mother of Pearl. In this activity we imitate the look of lacquerware using paper and paint.

Music for inspiration

Stilling Time: Traditional music of Vietnam Stilling Time Recordings

Vietnamese Zither by Tran Quang Hai

Vietnam: Poems and songs by Tran Van Khe

Traditional Music of Vietnam by Sounds of the World

You will need

Thick black paper, such as poster board, either 21cm x 30cm (9in x 12in) or 30cm x 42cm (12in x 18in)

Pencil

Scraps of shiny paper that look like Mother of Pearl

Scissors

Glue

Pearlescent (or gold, silver or copper) tempera paint

Small paint brushes

Permanent black fine line marker pen

What to do:

1) Decide what scene you want to depict in your 'lacquerware' picture. If you want it to look like a Vietnamese design you might choose a traditional idea, like goldfish or cranes, people wearing cone hats, boats on the water or scenery. You can choose any subject you like, including an abstract design.

2) Lightly sketch your design on the black poster board with a pencil.

3) On the back of your shiny paper draw shapes to represent pieces of Mother of Pearl. The shapes will become a part of the design you have drawn on your black board. Cut these out carefully and place them on the black background. Repeat this step until you have placed enough cut out shapes so that you begin to see your design take shape. Now glue these shapes so that all edges are lying flat.

4) Decide where and how you want to add paint. This will help define your picture. You might want to fill in small areas with colour and also add some delicate brush strokes.

5) When your picture is dry, you can add some outlines with the black marker pen. You can use it to define shapes so that they contrast with the black background, making your design resemble the lacquerware technique.

Unless otherwise specified, all location photographs by Jim Spates.

Artefact photography by Jan Regan.

Front cover. Three children, Scott McKinney.

Back cover. Hooded child, Frances Temple. Self-portrait, Alec Bullen, age 7.

Japan. p08, Mount Fuji, Images Colour Library.

Ecuador. p16, Otavalo, Lesley Mattson. p16, children, Scott McKinney. p17, plant, Lesley Mattson. p17, apartments, Scott McKinney. p18, Galapagos, Scott McKinney. p19, Otavalo, Lesley Mattson.

India. p25, poster of Gandhi, Chris Stowers, Panos Pictures. p28, lighting candles for Diwali, Simon Smith, Panos Pictures.

Russia. p30, shoreline, Raymond Steifel. p31, children, Raymond Steifel. p31, St Basil's Cathedral, Raymond Steifel. p32, urban housing, Moscow, Panos Pictures. p32, planting potatoes, Alexander Kuzmin. p33, chess players, M J O'Brien, Panos Pictures. p34, Fabergé egg, Kremlin Museums, Moscow, Bridgeman Art Library.

Turkey. p38, Alanya Castle, Şerif Yenen. p40, rug weaver, Deb Harris. p40, carpets, Deb Harris. p42, oya, Turkish Ministry of Culture. p42, illlustration of the tale of the Know-It-All Turban, Zeki Fındıkoğlu.

Kenya. p46, Masai women, Mariette Jackson. p47, baobab tree, Panos Pictures.

USA. p53, pumpkin patch, Frances Temple. p55, drummers, Jan Regan.

Vietnam. p58, rice worker in paddy field, Ian Harris. p61, houseboat, Ian Harris. p60, dragon sculpture, Deb Harris. p62, four water puppets, Ian Harris.

Maps by Andy Bone.

Milet Publishing Ltd
19 North End Parade
London W14 0SJ
England
Email: orders@milet.com
Website: www.milet.com

Picture the World: Children's Art around the Globe

First published by Milet Publishing Ltd in 2001
© Milet Publishing Ltd 2001
© Tracy Spates 2001

ISBN 1 84059 296 6

Edited by Mariette Jackson
Designed by Catherine Tidnam
Artworked by Catherine Tidnam and Mariette Jackson
Printed and bound in Slovenia by Midas